Friends

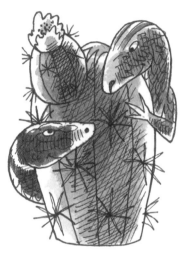

Snake
and
Lizard

Joy Cowley / Gavin Bishop

GECKO PRESS

First American edition published in 2011 by Gecko Press USA, an imprint of
Gecko Press Ltd.

A catalog record for this book is available from the US Library of Congress.

Distributed in the United States and Canada by
Lerner Publishing Group, Inc.
241 First Avenue North
Minneapolis, MN 55401 USA
www.lernerbooks.com

First published in 2009 by Gecko Press
PO Box 9335, Marion Square, Wellington 6141, New Zealand
Email: info@geckopress.com

Text © Joy Cowley
Illustrations © Gavin Bishop

© Gecko Press Ltd 2009

Design: Book Design Ltd, Christchurch, New Zealand
Printing: Everbest, China

ISBN hardback: 978-1-877579-01-1

For more curiously good books, please visit www.geckopress.com

For Terry who knows
that the best cure for an argument
is to forgive quickly,
then hug slowly.

Contents

Doors

It's true that when neighbors become good friends, walls can come down between houses. For Snake and Lizard, the houses were holes in the earth, and when the walls came down, the friends became the joint owners of a grand U-shaped burrow with two entrances.

Snake, who had a cautious nature, thought two doorways were better than one. If a fierce creature came through one entrance, she and Lizard could escape through the other. But one day, Snake found the second hole blocked with a thick sticky web in which sat a spider with furry legs and a body as big as an owl's egg.

Snake backed down the burrow as fast as she could slither and called for Lizard. 'There's a poisonous spider in our doorway!'

Lizard said calmly, 'It's quite harmless.'

Snake's tongue flickered. 'You knew it was there?'

Of course Lizard knew it was there. That cobweb was a storehouse of snacks. Several times he had helped himself to moths or flies. 'A spider has to build its house somewhere,' he said. 'We should make it feel at home, Snake. After all, we are professional helpers.'

Snake shivered. 'How can you talk like that? One bite and we'll be dead.'

'I told you, it's not venomous,' insisted Lizard. 'Oh, come on, Snake. A little compromise is in order.'

'Compromise,' repeated Snake.

'Yes. You know. We give a little. The spider gives a little.'

'Gives what?' said Snake.

Lizard was unwilling to admit that he had been stealing the spider's food. 'Elegance,' he said. 'Beautiful design. I'm talking about the web.'

'I know what you're talking about,' sniffed Snake. 'It's blocking our escape hole.'

Lizard waved his claws. 'We already have one good door. Let's think of the other as a window. We let the spider use this entrance, and in return, it spins us a very fine curtain. That, my friend, is a perfect example of compromise!'

Snake was not convinced. 'We don't have one good door. What we have is just an opening. That spider has to go.'

'Then let's get a door,' Lizard said quickly. 'If it makes you feel better, we'll find a strong door to match a window with a curtain.'

Snake by now was feeling sarcastic. 'Oh, yes, let's,' she hissed. "I suppose there are thousands of doors in the desert, crying, 'This one! This one!'"

Lizard blinked. 'Dear Snake, you are a genius! Of course there are thousands! Why didn't I think of that?'

Before Snake could say, 'Think of what?' Lizard was out of the burrow and scampering excitedly between clumps of Opuntia cactus. 'There! That one! No, that one's better!' He was pointing to the round fleshy stalks growing one on another. Each segment was roughly the shape of the entrance to the burrow, and each was bristling with prickles. 'What do you think?' he said triumphantly.

Snake-sight was not good, but then it didn't need to be. A cactus was a cactus. 'Too high, too tough, too sharp.'

'The perfect door!' squeaked Lizard.

Snake shook her head. 'Look Lizard, this solution has become a lot harder than the problem. All you have to do is get rid of the spider.'

'Oh, Snake! What happened to compromise?'

'Nothing happened to it,' hissed Snake. 'Compromise is a stupid word. I'm going back inside.' With that, she looped about and slipped into the burrow.

She went to the far entrance and, at a safe distance from the web, flicked her tongue and tasted spider in the air. Dimly, she saw its black shape against the light, and it filled her with fear. Lizard might be her best friend, she thought, but sometimes he had very silly ideas.

Eventually Snake heard familiar grunts and squeaks, and there was Lizard, dragging a disc of cactus stalk to the entrance. It was one he'd found on the ground, brown and dead but still armed with sharp prickles. 'Here is our door!' he announced breathlessly.

'Snake, you stay on the inside and hold it while I push it into place.'

Snake was tired of argument. As Lizard pushed the slab of cactus closer, she pressed her head to a patch without needles.

'Thank you,' said Lizard. His grunts and squeaks grew muffled as he hoisted the cactus. He had been right about the size. It fitted the burrow entrance so snugly that only a small rim of light showed around one edge.

Snake was suddenly in darkness. Now what happens? she wondered.

On the other side, Lizard was excited. 'It's perfect!' he cried. 'No one can get in. We're absolutely safe. Snake, I've made a door!'

Snake waited for the silence that followed. She smiled and waited some more.

'Snake? Are you there, Snake?'

'Yes.'

'Snake, I can't get in.'

Snake put her face to the strip of light. 'Get rid of the spider!' she yelled.

There was another silence, a longer one. 'Snake, dear, will you give the door a little push?'

Snake wanted to shout, 'No!' In fact, she wanted to say a lot of things, but Lizard sounded so anxious that all the words in her melted. She put her head against the door and pushed.

The round of cactus fell back with a plop and Snake was in sudden sunlight.

'Thank you, thank you, dear Snake!' Lizard, cheerful again, scuttled over the fallen door and into the burrow. 'Well now, it's a poor day when you don't discover something new, and I have just discovered an amazing thing about doors. They have to be either open or shut.'

'You mean they have no compromise?' asked Snake.

'That's it exactly,' said Lizard. 'Oh Snake, I knew you would understand.'

Window

Snake was deeply afraid of the spider that had spun a web over one of their entrances. Lizard tried to reason with her, but nothing he said could stop Snake from twitching in her sleep.

'I dreamed it poisoned us in the night,' she said.

'Trust me,' said Lizard. 'It's not a venomous spider.'

'Lizard, you don't know venomous,' Snake replied.

'In Australia, I have a very distant cousin called Taipan.

One bite can kill a hundred human things.'

Lizard scratched himself thoughtfully. 'How does she bite so many human things at once?'

Some questions were not worth answering. Snake said, 'Lizard, you allow a poisonous spider in our home, because it weaves a curtain for a window that's supposed to be a door. It doesn't make sense.'

Lizard scratched his pleasantly full belly. Every day the cobweb gave him a variety of food: flies, beetles, moths and, once, a very large cricket. The spider didn't seem to notice that bugs were disappearing. Perhaps it considered them fair rental for a web in someone else's doorway. 'Snake, I wonder if you have arachnophobia,' Lizard said gently. 'And before you ask, it means an unreasonable fear of spiders.'

'No. Definitely, I do not,' said Snake.

'I think you do,' said Lizard. 'It probably comes from your feelings of inferiority because you're a snake without venom. Have you ever considered that?'

Snake drew herself into a tight circle and tucked her head into her coils. 'I hate it when you are like this,' she said in a muffled voice.

'Like what?'

'Talking sideways,' she said. 'A poisonous spider
has blocked the entrance of my old burrow. I don't
want a window. I don't want a curtain. Either the
spider goes, or I do. You decide.'

Lizard was so upset that he wanted to say, 'Good, you
go'. But he couldn't. Of course he couldn't. Neither
could he bear to lose the insects caught in the web.
He sighed. Whatever his decision, he would lose.

There was only one small hope—to somehow convince Snake that the spider was harmless.

The opportunity came the next morning when they were warming themselves in the sun. Porcupine trotted along, rustling his quills and sniffing the ground for grubs. He stopped by Snake and Lizard. 'I see you've got a cobweb across your entrance.'

'It's a window,' Lizard said quickly.

'No it isn't,' said Snake.

Lizard nudged Snake. 'We're Helpers,' he said in a loud, professional voice. 'The spider needed a home, but Snake is worried that it might be venomous.'

'That spider?' Porcupine's quills rattled. 'No! Not a drop of venom in it.'

Snake put out her tongue and tested the air. She sensed that Porcupine was telling the truth. 'Are you sure?'

'It's about as toxic as a corncob,' said Porcupine who, like Snake and Lizard, sometimes visited the gardens of human things.

'Absolutely and utterly sure?' asked Snake.

Porcupine was offended. 'Are you telling me I don't know spiders?' he growled, and waddled away before he could get an answer.

Lizard realized that Snake still had doubts. He waved his claws at her. 'Well, that's one opinion. Let's check with our other neighbors. The squirrels will know. Likewise, the rats and rabbits. We should settle this little problem once and for all.'

By the end of the day, Snake may have been a little moody at being proved wrong, but she was sure, beyond argument, that the spider was harmless. All of the tension in her collapsed into tiredness.

Lizard, who was doubly talkative when happy,

had shifted his monologue from windows and curtains to a story about a homeless spider. He had convinced himself that it was their duty to offer shelter to a poor spider. But his talk was wasted on Snake. Exhausted by days and nights of fear, she had fallen into a deep sleep.

The next morning at first light, it was Lizard who was agitated. The spider's web, usually full of fluttering moths at this hour, had disappeared. The entrance was bare except for a few ragged strands that trembled in the breeze. There was no sign of the spider.

Lizard woke Snake to tell her the news. 'Gone!' he cried.

Snake stretched and yawned. 'It's moved on,' she suggested. 'Spiders don't settle for long.'

'All gone!' cried Lizard. 'Web as well! Do you know what this means?'

'No.'

'Something attacked it in the night—and I'm responsible! Oh, Snake, I betrayed it! Yesterday, I described that spider to—how many? It was probably one of the rats! Or Porcupine. No! Surely not my old friend Porcupine!'

Snake sighed. 'It's not your fault.'

'Yes it is! I practically gave them all an invitation!'

'No, you didn't,' Snake said soothingly. 'Look at it this way, Lizard. The problem is solved. We've got our entrance back.'

Lizard was too busy talking to listen. He switched from Lizard the Guilty to Lizard the Detective, and he ran to the open hole to look for footprints and other clues.

Snake didn't join him. She was still tired and planned to sleep all day. As she made herself comfortable, she wondered that one spider could cause so much fuss. She closed her eyes. Corncob, indeed! she thought. The spider might have been harmless, but it hadn't tasted all that good.

Rain Dance

The sky shimmered white and most of the desert creatures were sheltering from the sun. Even the scorpions had crawled under stones. The only moving things were two buzzards that circled at a great height, their eyes sharp for creatures dead or dying.

Snake and Lizard lay in their doorway under the hanging rock. Lizard began to describe the buzzards to Snake who could not see far. Then he remembered that Snake's mother had been eaten by a buzzard. Too late. A rippling sigh went through Snake and she collapsed into deep sadness.

Lizard drew closer. 'Snake dear, your mother had an excellent life. She lived to a great age.'

'True,' Snake said in a wobbly voice.

'Don't be sad she's gone. Just be happy she was your mother. Think of this, Snake. If she hadn't been your mother, I wouldn't be your friend.'

Snake thought, and said, 'What do you mean?'

Lizard waved his claws. 'No mother, no you, no us.'

Snake sighed again. 'You are right. My mother was excellent. Did I tell you she was also very powerful?'

'Yes, you did.'

'She knew so much serpent wisdom, so many earth secrets. I'm sure I didn't tell you how she created the dust storm.'

'You told me several times,' said Lizard quickly. Snake's stories about her mother made him feel irritable. With ninety-seven brothers and sisters, he didn't remember his own mother.

'On that afternoon she sang an earth song and thrashed her tail back and forth in the sand,' said Snake. 'The message went through earth and rock, and as it went it grew bigger and bigger. On the other side of the mountains it exploded out as a great dust storm.'

Lizard shrugged. 'What good did that do? I mean, if she'd sung a sky song and done a rain dance, I could understand. But a dust storm?'

Snake knew that Lizard was being unkind. She hissed back, 'So your mother knew how to do a rain dance?'

Lizard looked up at the buzzards, still soaring on high wind currents. 'I told you I never saw my mother,' he said in a hurt voice. He would have said more but he noticed beyond the buzzards a white cloud that had grown larger. It could well be a thunderhead. His heart beat bravely. 'I can do a rain dance,' he said.

Snake's head turned. 'You can?'

'Of course.'

Her eyes widened. 'All this time, Lizard, and you never mentioned it?'

The cloud above the horizon was definitely bigger and dark gray around its edges. 'I didn't think you were interested,' he said.

'Oh, but I am! Buddy, I'm your best friend. I'm interested in everything you do.'

He waited for her to say it.

'Go on. Do a rain dance for me. Please?'

At that moment, Lizard knew absolutely that he could do a real rain dance. He raised himself on his four solid legs, looked left and right, then walked out into the bright sun. Sky song, he thought. There had to be a sky song. He raised his head toward the large cloud that was far beyond Snake's vision and made squeaky noises. At the same time he stamped on the earth, front feet, then back feet. Tail twitching, he turned a half circle to face Snake, then he repeated the movements until he had no more song left in him.

Snake was impressed. 'I've never seen a rain dance before.'

'They're not very common,' Lizard admitted.

'It made my back shiver,' she said. 'You were so powerful, Lizard.'

Lizard glowed with pleasure. 'Thank you, dear Snake.'

'Is the rain going to come?'

He glanced at the sky. 'At any moment,' he said.

The rain, however, did not arrive. The cloud moved away and that night there was not even a misting of dew. The next day the sky grew white hot again, and Lizard explained to Snake the difference between sky songs and earth songs.

'Which is bigger?' he asked. 'Sky or earth?'

'I have never been able to work that out,' said Snake.

'Look around you, my friend. Earth is a flat circle, but up there, sky goes on forever. You must realize that your mother's dust-storm dance didn't have far to go.'

Snake nodded in agreement.

'Don't worry,' said Lizard. 'It will rain tomorrow.'

But it did not rain the next day. Or the next. If anything, the weather grew hotter.

'Clouds travel very slowly,' Lizard explained. 'Especially when they are heavy with rain. It might take them several days to get here.'

'If they are so far away, how did they hear your song?' Snake wanted to know.

'A powerful song travels anywhere,' Lizard replied.

The moon grew fat and then thin again, and still there was no change in the weather. After a while, Lizard stopped looking at the sky, and he and Snake talked of other things. Each felt that the word 'rain' could damage their friendship. Lizard was sure he had disappointed Snake. Snake thought she should not have repeated the story of her mother's dust dance. The friends were careful in their conversations and very kind to each other.

Two moons later, as they lay in the burrow, a great flash lit up the entrance. Soon after, the earth shook with a thunderous noise that was followed by a sound like pebbles dropping. At once, the smell of rain filled their home.

'The clouds have come!' cried Snake. 'Oh Lizard, you were right! They were heavy! Look at all that rain!'

Lizard walked to the entrance and gazed out at the solid lines of water falling. He nodded in satisfaction. 'You were right, too, Snake. It was a very powerful rain dance.'

The Hero

'Excuse me! Excuse me! Anyone in?' Porcupine's voice was as rough as two rocks rubbed together. His nose and eyes filled the doorway, blocking the light, and his quills rattled with impatience. 'Aren't you two supposed to be in the helping business?'

Snake and Lizard looked at their breakfast and waited.

Snake wanted to say, 'It's too early, we're not open yet.' But Porcupine bellowed, 'There's been a great tragedy!'

At once, Snake and Lizard were alert.

'What tragedy?' cried Lizard.

'Where?' said Snake.

'One of the jack rabbits,' said Porcupine, stepping back. 'He met a hero's death!'

Lizard and Snake squeezed out of the entrance together.

'Which rabbit?' Lizard demanded.

'A hero?' Snake said.

Porcupine said solemnly, 'It was none other than Ear Bent. He tried to stop a monster on the River of Death, just went out there, brave as you like, sat up on his hind legs and—'

'It trampled him?' Snake shivered with horror.

'They trampled him,' said Porcupine. 'A whole herd of monsters, one after the other. Left him flatter than a shadow.'

Lizard's eyes bulged. 'Eek!' he squeaked. 'Poor Ear Bent! Oh my, oh my!'

Snake moved back toward the burrow. 'If he's—he's—we can't help him, I'm afraid.'

Porcupine shook his long needles. 'Of course you can't help him. It's his family. Tomorrow morning the rabbits will have a Gathering to release Ear Bent's spirit. They think it right that Snake and Lizard, Helper and Helper, should speak at his Gathering. They sent me to ask you.'

Snake began, 'I don't think we—'

Lizard added, 'Usually we don't—'

'They will double your fee,' said Porcupine. 'Four quails' eggs and four beetles.'

'In this case,' said Lizard, 'because he is a hero—'

'It would be a pleasure,' said Snake quickly. Then she added, 'I mean it would be an honor.'

'Honor is right,' said Porcupine. 'Never before, in desert history, has a creature tried to stop these savage monsters. Ear Bent may have lost his life, but overnight he has become a legend. You will see to it that his spirit has a fitting send-off.' Porcupine shook himself again, with a noise like a storm in dry leaves. 'Tomorrow at sun-up,' he reminded them as he walked away.

For a while, Snake and Lizard didn't speak or move. There were many jack rabbits and they had seen Ear Bent only once or twice, but now they felt they knew him intimately.

'Flatter than a shadow,' Snake whispered, and they both shuddered.

'No one escapes the monsters,' Lizard said.

'Except Skunk,' said Snake.

Lizard remembered Skunk who had crossed the River of Death to meet his beloved. They had heard from a turtle that a buzzard had seen Skunk, his mate and three young skunks on the other side.

The friends were quiet again, imagining flattened fur

on the hard dark surface, seeing the monsters roaring over it again and again. Eventually Lizard said, 'What kind of creature kills but does not eat?'

'Truly they are monstrous,' said Snake. She looked at Lizard. 'Tell me, what do the monsters eat?'

Lizard thought for a long time. He hated saying that he didn't know, but that was the truth. 'We shouldn't waste time talking about them, Snake. We need to plan speeches for the Gathering. Think of the courage in the heart of this ordinary rabbit.'

'Ordinary on the outside, extraordinary on the inside,' agreed Snake.

'Compassionate, a martyr to the cause,' said Lizard. 'Ear Bent saw desert creatures killed on the River of Death, and he knew something had to be done to stop the monsters. He stood there, without a thought for his own safety.'

'Fearless,' said Snake.

'A great hero,' said Lizard.

Snake raised her head and said passionately, 'His story will be passed down through the generations. No one will ever forget what Ear Bent did.' She

lowered her head and murmured in Lizard's ear,
'But actually, don't you think—'

'He was an absolute idiot!' Lizard said firmly.

They nodded in agreement and went back into the
burrow to finish their breakfast.

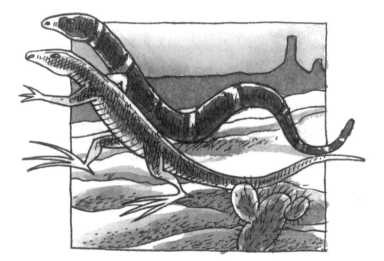

The Gathering

It was part of animal law that when there was a Gathering, all creatures were safe. Buzzards and coyotes sat at a distance, heads lowered in respect. The doves had no fear of the desert falcon, and Snake slid past a family of mice with her eyes averted. She could not even allow herself to taste their scent in the air.

The morning was still cool, the shadows long and

pale. Recent rains had covered sand and rock with a carpet of green, already flowering. In a few days the new growth would wither in the hot sun and drop seeds for the next rain months away. But now, on this morning of the Gathering, the desert was a dramatic green splashed with every other shade imaginable.

'The blossoming earth pays tribute to Ear Bent,' said Porcupine who always managed to make conversation sound like an important announcement.

Snake hissed in Lizard's ear. 'Ear Bent, my tail! It's a tribute to the power of your rain dance, Lizard.'

'Of course,' Lizard replied. 'But if Porcupine wants to make Ear Bent's family feel proud, we must not take it from them.'

Snake thought about that. 'All right. We'll let Ear Bent have the credit.'

'It's what Helpers do,' added Lizard.

There were more creatures present than anyone could count. They had gathered around the low slope inhabited by the family of the great hero. The air was so filled with squeaks, chirps, grunts, howls, whistles, scuffles and growls that Porcupine could not make himself heard and he had to ask Coyote to howl for silence. When everyone settled down, Porcupine stood tall on his hind feet, nose in air, and introduced the famous Helpers who would give the solemn speeches, Snake first, then Lizard.

Snake had not counted on speaking first. She had been watching the rows of baby mice, frogs and small birds in the front row, and her mouth was so full of juice that when she opened it, she dribbled and splashed, much to her embarrassment. But speak she did, and very well, too. 'No animal present here would walk, hop, slither or run across the River of Death. Not one of us would dare to challenge the monsters who kill without purpose. Only Ear Bent had the courage to do that. We honor him today and wish his spirit the speed of the wind.'

There were squeaks and snorts of agreement, and then it was Lizard's turn. Snake watched her Buddy with admiration. What a great speaker he was, so full of emotion. If he exaggerated a little, that was surely allowed at a time like this.

'Ever since the first jack rabbit was born, rabbits

have had a reputation for being gentle, being meek.' Lizard shut his eyes and shook with pretended fear. 'They were known not as fighters but as runaways.'

Snake was puzzled. If the first rabbit born was the first rabbit, who was its mother?

'Then along came Ear Bent to show the world what rabbits are really made of. Hearts as strong as mountains! Courage wider than the desert! One rabbit stood alone on the River of Death so that all rabbits would have new respect. Let the rest of us bow low to Ear Bent's family.'

Lizard's speech was so passionate that most creatures turned and bowed to the large rabbit family who looked awkward and a little surprised. Even Snake, who thought that Lizard was going too far, raised her head and lowered it toward the grass which still smelled of rain.

Oddly enough, it was Gray Run, Ear Bent's mate, who was least impressed with Lizard's talk and all the bowing and scraping. 'That's very nice, but who is going to carry on with Ear Bent's work? Which of you is going to do something about those monsters?'

35

There was a shuffling in the crowd, a nervous twitch of fur and feathers, followed by a long silence.

Gray Run went on in her high, sharp voice. 'Come on, then! Who's it to be?'

Porcupine said gruffly, 'We cannot start any important campaign without a plan. We'll think about it. In a few moons we'll call a meeting.'

The rabbit gave a shrill squeal that could have been laughter or anger. 'Just as I thought! None of you has an ounce of Ear Bent's courage. Let me tell you, my Ear Bent's spirit will not leave until someone else takes on his work.'

No one wanted to hear this. If Ear Bent's spirit didn't travel on to the spirit world, it would try to find a home here. No one wanted a restless rabbit ghost in its nest or burrow or lair.

'It's impossible!' snapped a turtle. 'Nothing can stop the monsters.'

A buzzard that flew far and saw much said that she had once seen the monsters stopped by rocks. 'There were giant stones across the River of Death.'

'How did they get there?' Porcupine demanded.

'They fell down a cliff,' said the buzzard. 'The monsters didn't come back for many days.'

'You were there for days?' questioned Porcupine.

The buzzard shrugged her dusty wings. 'There was so much food on the road. We could eat it without getting trampled.'

No one wanted to talk about that, and some small animals moved away from the buzzard.

A turtle stretched out its neck. 'So how do we make rocks fall from a cliff?'

An idea jumped into Snake's head like a brilliant light, and she could not keep it to herself. 'Lizard can do it!' she cried. 'His rain dance brought the rain storm. He can do a rock dance to bring down rocks.'

'A rock dance?' Lizard stared at her. 'Where did you get that idea? I don't like rocks. Rocks don't like me. I do sky—not earth!' But most of his words were drowned by great cheers from the Gathering. The quails skittered about, cackling with excitement, while the rabbit family rubbed their paws together and squeaked through their long front teeth.

'He can do it!' Snake announced. 'Lizard can do anything!'

Lizard didn't know whether he wanted to stuff a cactus in Snake's mouth, or believe her. Maybe she was right. Maybe he could do a rock dance and bring down a heap of stones on the River of Death.

Now all the creatures were chanting, 'Rock dance! Rock dance! Rock dance!' and Lizard felt powerful with their energy. It was like the hatching of an egg.

A small idea, going nowhere, had suddenly burst open and become a living thing. Yes, yes! He would do a rock dance. He would finish the jack rabbit's work, stop the monsters and save the desert.

'Rock dance! Rock dance!' Even the buzzards were calling with gritty voices.

Lizard took a deep breath. Tails and scales! He, Lizard, of Lizard and Snake, Helper and Helper, would save the world!

Rock Dance

The creatures chanted all the way to the River of Death which lay flat and gray, spotted here and there with patches of dried blood, feathers and fur. The gathering was not sure which scrap of fur belonged to Ear Bent. In the early morning light it was hard to tell, and no one wanted to get too close—especially not Lizard. He had already decided that he would do his rock dance to one side of the

River of Death, where it wound between two cliffs. There, on each side, rocks were piled high, round and rusty brown. Although they resembled solid walls, a very good rock dance would probably bring those stones tumbling down.

The chanting was drowned by a roaring sound. The earth shook, and all the creatures fled into the fringe of desert scrub. Only Snake and Lizard were still at the edge of the river when the monster rushed toward them. This was a giant, as high as the cliffs, and with many huge feet. With blazing eyes it rushed past, its breath sweeping Lizard and Snake back in a double somersault. Then it was gone.

Lizard got up, shook himself and said in a loud voice, 'I will now do the rock dance.'

The army of creatures crept out of the desert scrub behind him, rabbits first, then green winder snakes, rattlers, lizards, a coyote, frogs, rats, porcupines and buzzards. Bent Ear's mate Gray Run showed her long narrow teeth. 'You are doing the dance here?'

'Of course,' said Lizard.

'Not on the River of Death?' she said.

'It's a rock dance,' Lizard said with great dignity. 'A rock dance is done near rocks.'

Gray Run clacked her teeth at him. 'You're afraid.'

Before Lizard could answer, Snake raised her head and hissed at Gray Run, who jumped back, eyes wide. Snake hissed again. 'Afraid?' she whispered. Then Snake went close and put her face against Lizard's. 'You can do it.'

This was one of those times when Lizard's cold blood felt quite warm. He nodded, lifted his head and stamped in the dirt. His voice went up in a thread of sound that was soon drowned as the others crowded around him, chanting, 'Rock dance! Rock dance! Rock dance!'

Gray Run folded her paws and chose not to sing.

Lizard had never felt so powerful. He knew that this was the supreme moment of his life, the reason for which he had been born. He was like a great warrior surrounded by hundreds of foot soldiers. Even the buzzards and coyotes were working for him: the coyotes with muzzles to the sky, howling their support, the buzzards shaking their dusty wings and clacking their beaks. What a noise filled the air!

'Rock dance! Rock dance!'

The chanting was so loud that they didn't hear the next monster. It was smaller than the first, bright blue with gleaming eyes and four round feet. As it came around the corner, it swerved toward them.

The chanting faded. All the birds flew into the air, squawking. Then the monster swerved back, across the middle line of the river. Lizard stopped his dance and stared as it went headfirst into the cliff on the other side. Crash! Rocks fell, big rocks, one after the other! Round and brown, they rolled like giant eggs over the monster, through the scrub and across the river. They sounded full of thunder. By the time they stopped rolling, most of the animals had disappeared, racing back to their lairs and burrows, chattering with fear.

Lizard was too stunned to move, and Snake wouldn't leave him. 'D-d-danger!' she stuttered. 'R-r-run!'

Lizard could make only the smallest squeak. This was the first time he had seen a monster close up. It was injured. One of its eyes, peering out from the

rocks, was broken, and its breath came out in clouds
of steam.

Snake nudged him. 'G-g-go!' she urged.

Lizard found his voice. 'It's not dangerous. I killed it!
Snake, my rock dance killed it!'

As he spoke, the monster's dented side fell open, and
out of its blue stomach came a—

'Human thing!' they said together.

It was a human he-thing. It stood on the River of Death, scratching its head fur as it looked at the dead monster and the rocks. Then slowly, still scratching its fur, the human thing walked toward Snake and Lizard.

That made them move. Quick as a whip, Snake slipped through the scrub with Lizard scampering at her side. When they were sure they had not been followed, they stopped in the shade of a big old barrel cactus to catch their breath.

'There was really no danger,' said Lizard. 'The human thing wanted to thank me for saving his life,' said Lizard. 'I helped him to escape from the monster.'

'Maybe,' said Snake. 'Maybe he just wondered where everyone had gone. Not many human things get to see so many animals in one place.'

Lizard was disappointed. There were times when Snake did not appreciate him, and although he tried not to mind, the rock dance had been so successful, he felt he was entitled to a small sulk.

Snake said soothingly, 'Lizard? I said you could do it.'

For Lizard, that wasn't enough. He turned away.

Snake edged closer. 'I don't know how many rock dances there have been, but there was never one as good as yours.' She put her head on his. 'And there never will be again. You looked like a great dragon!'

Lizard felt much better. 'Bent Ear's spirit deserved a good send-off,' he said with a modest wave of his claws. Then emotion overcame him and he jumped high in the air. 'Oh Snake! What a morning! What excitement! What discovery!'

'Discovery?' murmured Snake.

Lizard's eyes were shining. 'Now we know what the monsters eat.'

Then they said together, 'Human things!'

Sister Forty-Nine

By mid-sun the following day, giant river monsters came in to pick up the fallen rocks and haul away their dead friend. On the third day, the River of Death was clear again, streaming with the hard-skinned creatures that rushed and roared as though nothing had happened.

In the depth of her coils, Snake felt relief. Lizard had received more attention than was good for him.

He had taken to walking on his hind legs, head in air, ordering other animals, including Snake, to bring him food. He also claimed that he had inherited the powerful rock dance from his dragon ancestors who could bring down entire mountains. He even claimed that he, Lizard, could make a mountain fall flat on its face.

It was all a bit much for Snake who secretly believed that the rocks had fallen when the blue monster crashed into the cliff. The monster had lost its way because it was greatly surprised, and the great surprise had come from seeing so many desert animals gathered in one place. But there was no way Snake could present this explanation to her friend. She knew, however, that time marched through the desert like a tortoise, slowly but surely, leaving some things behind and bringing new things to consider. The River of Death was cleared, the monsters returned, and Lizard's admirers drifted away.

Life for Snake and Lizard, Helper and Helper, had almost returned to normal when the visitor arrived. They heard her screeching down the burrow, 'Twenty-Three? Oh yes, you're in there, Twenty-Three—and so is that reptile.'

Lizard squealed with fright.

'Are you number twenty-three in your family?' Snake asked.

Lizard gulped. 'Y-yes, and th-th-that is Sister Forty-Nine.'

'Buddy, you have ninety-seven brothers and sisters. How do you know which one it is?'

'Twenty-Three!' The voice rattled like hailstones. 'Do I have to come in there and get you?'

Lizard shook from nose to tail. 'It's her voice! She's crossed days of desert to find me!'

'She knew where we were living?'

'S-s-someone must have t-t-told her!'

Snake understood. News of the rock dance had spread far and wide. She sighed. 'You'd better go and see what she wants.'

'I can't! Oh Snake, she's the bully in the family. She used to bite our tails. Please, dear friend, go and talk to her.'

Snake was not brave, and at that moment she felt

very protective of her tail. 'It's your sister,' she said firmly. 'You go!'

While they argued back and forth, the voice grew louder. Sister Forty-Nine was coming down the burrow. She made so much noise that Snake expected a very large lizard. In fact, she was no bigger than her brother, but clearly she had a very nasty temper.

'It's true!' she screeched. 'Oh yes, true as daylight! A snake and a lizard in the same burrow, no less. Never, I told Sister Eighty-Six. Not in our family. A snake? A dirt-creeping lizard-eater? Brother Twenty-Three, I have come to take you away!'

'I don't eat lizards,' Snake said, trying not to remember the old days. 'We work together. We run a helping business.'

'We are friends,' said Lizard in a quivering voice.

Sister Forty-Nine thrust her sharp little nose at him. 'Oh yes, let me guess. Friend one day, dinner the next! Wake up, Twenty-Three! Lizards and snakes do not work together. Not in all creation! Enough of this mess! Oh yes! I'm here to save you, brother. I'm taking you back to our family!'

Lizard squirmed under her sharp claws. 'Sister! You don't understand!' But while Lizard was shaking with fear, his sister was trembling with rage. She had changed color, her neck and chest flushed dark red.

Snake slid closer and said in her kindest helping voice, 'Let us all calm down and talk about this.'

'Don't you come near me!' snarled Sister Forty-Nine, showing a row of sharp teeth. 'I know your kind of low-slung life.'

'I think you have an anger problem,' Snake said pleasantly. 'Perhaps I can help you to change that.'

'You help me?' Sister Forty-Nine screeched. 'You— you legless worm!'

While Snake saw herself as a peacemaker, she accepted that there were some insults beyond forgiveness. She uncoiled and rose until her back was almost against the roof of the burrow, her head directly over Sister Forty-Nine. Then she gave a long and magnificent HISS-SS-SS-SS!

There was instant change. The sister's mouth closed. Her eyes opened wide. She let go of her brother and shrank back against the wall.

Lizard rushed back to Snake and yelled at his sister, 'Go! Get out of here! Leave us alone!'

That's exactly what she did. Like all bullies, she

was not brave beneath her teeth and claws. She disappeared from the burrow without another sound.

Lizard was still shaking like an aspen leaf. 'How dare she say those terrible things! Oh Snake! I'm so sorry!'

Snake coiled around him to soothe his trembling legs. 'Did you notice that she was quite highly colored? I wonder if your family has chameleon blood.'

'She goes red when she loses her temper,' said Lizard. 'She's always been like that. She has a very excitable nature.'

'Like you,' Snake murmured.

'What?'

'Nothing.'

But Lizard jumped up and twirled in a dance that had nothing to do with rocks or rain. 'I heard you! How can you say I'm like her? I'm not! I'm not! You're supposed to be my friend!'

'So I am, dear Buddy,' said Snake soothingly. 'Come on. Let's go and find some lunch.'

Life Cycle

Lizard and Snake enjoyed their morning rambles which they called withers.

'Walk?' Lizard once suggested.

'I don't walk,' Snake reminded him. 'I was made to slither.'

'We should find a compromise word,' said Lizard. 'What do you think of wither?'

Snake had never thought of wither, but the idea of

having a word that served them both appealed to her. So wither it was.

The clear light of a new day always put them in a talking mood, and they never ran out of things to discuss, which is why they sometimes withered further than they intended. On this particular morning, they went all the way to the salt flats where nothing grew and patches of white salt reflected the sun. At the edge of the flats lay a rusty bicycle without tires or handlebars.

When the friends were sure that it was not some kind of trap, they went close, and Lizard put his front legs on one of the rusted rims. He hopped back when the wheel turned. 'What is this thing?'

Snake, who could not see as well as Lizard, tasted the air with her flickering tongue. Salt, iron, rock, nothing living. She nudged the wheel and again it moved. She turned to push the other. It also turned. This was a thing of the desert, Snake decided, trying to remember all the desert wisdom passed on by her mother. It was—it was—. Some words came together inside her. 'Lizard, we've found a life cycle!'

'Ah—I know that.' Lizard stood tall. 'I knew that all along. I just forgot how it works.'

'It measures the cycle of life,' Snake said.

'Yes. I remember now. The hatchings and dyings.'

'Bigger than that,' said Snake, who was clearly hearing her mother's voice inside her. 'It's the way of all creatures in the desert. The worm gets eaten by the bird, and the worm becomes the bird. The snake eats the bird and the bird becomes the snake. Along comes the coyote to eat the snake. Snake is now coyote. But coyote dies and his breath goes off to the spirit land. Along come worms and they eat the dead coyote.'

She put her head on the ground and slid a little way under the wheel to examine the spokes. 'It is indeed a wonderful life cycle. See all these counting rods? They represent the creatures—worms, birds, snakes, coyotes.'

'What about lizards?'

'Oh.' Snake realized that her mother had not mentioned lizards. 'You'll be there somewhere, Buddy.'

Lizard sniffed. 'You made all that stuff up.'

'No, I didn't. My mother told me.'

'It's just a story,' Lizard insisted.

'But it's a true story,' said Snake.

They were about to spoil the morning with an

argument when a dark gray head popped out of a nearby hole. 'What are you two doing here?' demanded a large salt-flat rat.

'None of your business,' said Lizard.

'Oh, yes it is,' said the rat. 'This is my patch and I'm trying to sleep.'

'I'm sorry,' said Snake. 'My friend doesn't understand how this life cycle measures life in the desert. I was trying to explain how large eats small and then the smallest eats the largest—'

'What are you on about?' The rat pushed a wheel. 'This here is a bike. It carries human things when their legs don't work. Now you two scram and leave me in peace!'

The rat was big and its fur was standing on end. It was definitely time to go. Snake and Lizard backed off, turned, and withered away with as much dignity as they could manage.

'Rats are ignorant creatures,' Snake said.

Lizard looked straight ahead and said in a distant voice, 'Now I know how the life cycle works. Worms are eaten by lizards. The lizard is grabbed by a hungry chicken. The chicken is food for the human thing. Human thing dies and goes back to being worms. End of story is beginning of story.'

Snake thought about this. 'It's not what my mother said.'

'Beg your pardon, Snake, but your mother didn't know everything.'

They went on without speaking, giving Snake time to think some more. Lizard's theory sounded reasonable, yet Snake knew that her mother's teaching had been true. How could this be?

The sun was now halfway up the sky and they were glad to get back to the shade of sage brush and cactus. Suddenly, Snake stopped. 'Lizard!' she called.

Lizard turned.

'You! Me! We're both right!' she said. 'There are two true stories!'

'There are?'

'Yes, yes! That's why the life cycle has two round things!'

Lizard stared at her. 'Of course! Snake, dear, your cleverness always surprises me.'

After that, they chatted excitedly about the marvelous life cycle that held together the true stories of all snakes and all lizards.

They agreed that it was the best wither they'd had in a long, long time.

Skin

The news spread quickly by wing and paw. There were two human things in the desert. They lived in a thin yellow burrow by the river.

The burrow had come out of a cocoon, Porcupine declared. Yes, definitely a cocoon. The human things shook the burrow then pinned it to the earth where it flapped in the afternoon breeze like a great yellow butterfly going nowhere. Come sunset, the human things crawled inside their burrow and didn't come out until morning.

The animals jittered at the news. Human things could not be trusted. They had been known to feed an animal one day, then kill it the next, with no good reason for either.

The only exception to this was the human she-thing who lived at the edge of the desert. Snake and Lizard visited occasionally to collect eggs from her chicken house and the fat green beetles that swarmed in her garden. That particular human thing appeared safe since she had no cats or dogs and her only weapon was the brush stick she used to sweep the yard. As far as Snake was concerned, all other human creatures were ahead of coyotes and buzzards on the list of extreme dangers. At least buzzards and coyotes were predictable.

Lizard's talk of going to the river to see the yellow burrow made Snake feel as though she had eaten a frog that was still hopping inside her. Her answer was a rippling shudder that ended in a clear, 'No!'

But Lizard, as always, tried to change her mind.

67

'We'll be on the other side of the river.'

Snake shuddered again. 'Porcupine said the human things are as tall as trees. The river is not tall. They can walk across it.'

'True, the river is shallow but in the middle it runs fast. By the time they waded across, we'd be back in our burrow.'

'No,' said Snake. 'Definitely not.'

'We'll be absolutely safe.'

'No, no, no!'

'Please, dear friend!'

'Not until the desert turns to ice,' Snake replied.

But in fact, the day was very hot when they left the burrow, walking and slithering—withering—toward the river. Because the sun had melted snow on the distant mountains, the river was wide, and as Lizard had mentioned, the water in its middle sang in white waves. The vastness of the river and the smallness of the yellow tent made Snake bold. She raised her head high. 'I don't see any human things.'

'They are sitting beside their burrow,' said Lizard. 'Two of them, a she-thing and a he-thing. Now they are standing up. Oh Snake! They are—yes, yes!'

'Yes what?'

'They are shedding their skins!'

Snake rippled with interest. She was an authority on skin-shedding and had heard many rumors about human things, how they actually made the skins that they shed every day. She struggled to see beyond blurred movement. 'Tell me! Tell me!' she cried.

Lizard stood on hind legs, balancing on his tail. 'This is so interesting! They are peeling skin off in pieces— their stomachs, their feet. Now their legs! Oh my! This is amazing!'

'What is it?'

'Snake, I have never seen this before. They are pink and bare—like newborn mice! They've come to the edge of the river, side by side.'

Snake twitched. 'Walking across!'

'No, no. They are leaning down, washing themselves. What a rare sight! What a discovery. Snake, this is the first time I've understood why human things are not like us creatures. It's because they've failed!'

'Failed?' Snake's tongue flickered, testing the air.

Yes, she could taste human things, water, and the familiar energy of Lizard. 'Failed at what?'

'Oh, my friend! This is something your mother didn't tell you!'

Snake grew impatient. 'What do you mean?'

'I'm talking about fur,' he replied. 'It's not just head and face. They have small patches on their bodies. We were wrong, Snake. We thought that human things made skins to show us their power. It's not so. They tried to grow fur, and they couldn't. Not all over. They make skins to cover their shame!'

Snake thought about her own skin, new and soft, emerging naturally as she shed the old. 'Human things are not natural,' she said.

'Utterly unnatural,' agreed Lizard. 'So why are they here? That is the question I ask. Why are they not with their own herds in their own lands?'

After the bathing, the he-thing and she-thing went inside the yellow burrow, leaving their skins on the riverbank. There was nothing more to see but, according to Lizard, there was a great deal to be done. He and Snake hurried home with a discovery that excited them but also confirmed their suspicions. Human things were coming to the desert.

'We know,' said Lizard, 'that they spread across land and nothing stops them.'

'The monsters eat them,' said Snake, remembering

the human thing that had staggered out of the belly of the blue monster on the River of Death.

'They still thrive,' Lizard replied. 'That yellow burrow is the first sign of an invasion. It is our duty to do something, Snake, or the desert will be filled with yellow burrows.'

Snake's nervous twitch came back. 'You're not—not planning to chase them out.'

'Oh dear, no!' Lizard laughed. 'We are helpers, Snake. We don't use violent solutions to fix problems. This matter can be resolved peacefully by law. We'll simply draw up a list of the skin types that are permitted to live in the desert.'

'Snakeskin,' said Snake quickly. 'And lizard skin.'

'Fur and feathers,' said Lizard.

'Scales,' added Snake.

Lizard scratched his head with one claw. 'What about insects? Some have scales, some don't.'

'All insect skin,' said Snake.

'And no unnaturals,' Lizard said firmly.

'Definitely no unnaturals,' said Snake.

With their list in place, Lizard decided they should visit a jack rabbit who was known for his dislike of human things. 'Of all creatures,' said Lizard, 'he is the best to make our list public. By evening everyone will know and by tomorrow it will be desert law.'

'What if the human things break the law?' Snake asked.

'One thing at a time,' said Lizard. 'First, we have to make it.'

Lizard was right about the rabbit, who was off like a bolt of lightning, bounding through the desert, shouting the new skin-type proposal at every lair, nest and burrow.

'Agreed!' twittered the birds.

'Absolutely!' chattered the squirrels.

Snake and Lizard glowed with goodness. This, surely, was their greatest achievement. Their list would save the desert for desert creatures, and result in a law that would carry their reputation as Helper and Helper through all animal history.

As they settled in the burrow that night, they congratulated each other.

'You are an excellent planner, Lizard,' Snake said.

'It was your idea, dear Snake,' Lizard replied. 'You said human things were not natural, remember?'

These pleasant thoughts would have continued but for the sudden rumpus outside the burrow. There was a sound like dry leaves in a storm, and a rough voice shouted, 'All right, you two! Who's responsible for that list?'

Snake froze. 'Porcupine!' she whispered. 'You forgot quills!'

'You mean, you forgot,' Lizard replied.

'It wasn't my list,' she said quickly.

The angry rattling went on. 'I demand to know why

I've been classified as unnatural.'

Snake began to shiver. 'He's furious!'

'It's all right,' said Lizard. 'He's too big to get in.'

'That's not the point,' Snake said. 'It was a mistake. You need to go out there and explain.'

'I can't,' said Lizard, then, in a drowsy voice, he added, 'I'm asleep.'

Love

Knowing how much Snake liked to eat chicken eggs, Lizard sometimes visited the chicken house on the human thing's farm to fetch a gift for his friend. This was no easy task.

The farm was on the edge of the desert, a long walk from the burrow, and the hole under the chicken house was small. Rolling a large egg back through desert scrub was hard work. But it wasn't the effort that Lizard minded. It was the way Snake swallowed the egg whole. She didn't even taste it. She opened her mouth with a 'Thank you,' and his morning's work disappeared in an instant.

He had to say something about it.

'But Lizard,' she protested. 'I always swallow eggs whole.'

'I know. That's why I am telling you how I feel. I hope you'll forgive me, dear Snake, but I—' He took a deep breath. 'I feel you don't quite appreciate my gift.'

Snake looked surprised. 'I do appreciate it! I appreciate you, Buddy! I absolutely LOVE eggs! You know that.'

Lizard was not comforted. 'You mean you like eggs. We do not use the word love for food.'

'I do.'

'Love,' said Lizard, 'is a word for relationships, not for things. You can't have a relationship with your dinner.'

'I can,' Snake replied.

'No, no! Let me explain!' Lizard spoke slowly. 'I fully understand that fresh chicken eggs are your

very favorite meal. That's why I get them for you.
But you don't love fresh chicken eggs. What you
experience is a serious case of like.'

'Oh,' said Snake.

'Some words are special. Have you listened to the
silly way most desert creatures talk about love? They
love morning light, they love their nests, they love to
feel safe or well fed. But do they use the love word for
each other or themselves? No, they don't! Snake! Are
you listening?'

Snake made a small noise that could have been yes or no.

'If you use words carelessly, they lose their meaning,' said Lizard. 'I thought your mother, that serpent of all wisdom, would have told you as much.'

Snake's tail twitched and Lizard realized he had gone too far. He said in a softer voice, 'Love is a word for friends to share. Don't you agree? You are my best friend, Snake, and I love you.'

Snake was quiet.

Lizard moved so that he could see her face. 'Friends should love each other. Do you love me?'

There was another twitch and eventually Snake looked at him. 'It's a serious case of like,' she said.

LOSS

It was not the first time that Lizard had criticized Snake for the way she swallowed food whole. She felt hurt. No, she was not sulking. She simply needed some quiet time to consider important subjects like life and chicken eggs.

As for Lizard, he could not bear her silences, and he filled the burrow with cheerful words arranged as questions. Snake didn't answer. Finally, he said in an important voice, 'I am going for a walk.'

When he said walk instead of wither, Snake realized he meant to go by himself. Good, she thought. I'll get some peace.

'I won't be back until midday,' he added, as he stomped off, nose in the air.

For a while, Snake enjoyed the quiet. It soothed the spiky feelings inside her and gave her space to think about other things. She tidied the burrow and then lay coiled at the entrance under the overhanging rock, watching the sun climb toward midday. The problem with Lizard, she decided, was that he always wanted her to be like him. She needed to be firm. Firm but gentle. When he returned they would have a friendly talk and she would ask him to respect who she was—a snake and not a legless lizard.

The sun came to the high point in the sky and shadows became small dark puddles. Lizard had not returned. A new spiky feeling started at Snake's tail and worked its way up to her throat. It was not like Lizard to be late. Something had happened.

Her first thought was that he could have grown tired

of her silence and found another burrow, but that was not like Lizard. Something—dare she think it?—something had happened to him.

The spiky feeling grew worse as Snake counted all the dangers that the desert offered a brave but defenseless lizard. In the eye of her mind, she saw a coyote swallowing Lizard whole. She saw a buzzard with the tip of Lizard's tail dangling from its sharp beak. Every time she imagined these things, a groan rippled through her.

The sun slid down the other side of the sky and tucked itself into an orange bed on the horizon. Now the shadows of cacti were long fingers on the earth, and evening insects filled the air. It was time to go back into the burrow but still Snake lingered, tasting the air with her flickering tongue, wishing she had the sharp sight of a bird.

Where was he?

The orange strip of sunset paled to yellow and disappeared as the first stars appeared. Bats came out of hiding and darted after insects. An owl hooted nearby. It was danger time. Snake had to slide back into the burrow, but oh, what a different burrow it was, a dark hole, cold with emptiness.

Snake was now convinced that something terrible had happened to Lizard. She was also aware that she had not said goodbye. She had been angry with him. How could she have been so cold? He was kind, clever, brave, always good to her! He was her own dear Buddy. She rocked with the pain of remembering all the unpleasant words and equally unpleasant silences she had inflicted on him. If only she had been nice, he would not have gone off on his own and—and—Oh! Oh!

Painful thoughts were exhausting but Snake could not sleep. Now, more than ever, she needed her mother's wise advice. But she suspected that her mother would have said something like, 'It's your fault. You did not appreciate him and now it is too late.'

'I'm alone in the world!' Snake cried. 'All alone! Why was I so cruel?'

A ladder of pale light in the burrow told her that morning had come. She slid past Lizard's empty sleeping space and out to the cool desert where the sun was waking up, stretching over the distant mountains.

Snake felt ill with worry and lack of sleep. She would have to organize a desert search for information. Someone would know something. Then there would have to be a Gathering to send Lizard's spirit on its way. This thought was too much for Snake. She was shaking with wild sobs when a loud voice cried, 'I've been a prisoner!'

There was Lizard beside her, dirt on his face and claws.

'You—you—' She was still hiccuping from her sobs.

'The chicken house!' said Lizard. 'I went to get you another egg! While I was rolling it out of the nest, the human thing blocked the hole with a big stone. I couldn't get out! I've spent all night digging. I'm exhausted!'

'The chicken house!' Snake found her voice. 'You didn't tell me!'

'It was going to be a surprise,' said Lizard. 'But I had to leave the egg behind. The hole wasn't big enough. Oh Snake, I'm so tired!'

'You are tired! What do you think it's been like for me?'

'You were here,' said Lizard. 'You weren't digging for your life.'

Snake felt a hiss coming on. 'You selfish, thoughtless creature! You've no idea! I could have died with worry! You didn't say where you were going. How was I to know—'

'You weren't talking to me,' Lizard said in a huffy voice.

'I was listening!'

'Well, listen now! I went to the chicken house to get you another surprise and I ended up locked in with seven hungry chickens! Think about it! I had to hide in the straw until they went to sleep. All night, it was scratch, scratch, scratch, to make a new hole. When at last I get home, all you can do is hiss at me!'

'Oh, yes! You, you, you! It's all about you, isn't it!' cried Snake. 'That's typical! You never spare a thought for anyone else!'

Lizard's eyes grew large with anger. 'I don't eat chicken eggs!' he squeaked. 'I don't swallow them whole!'

They could have had a spectacular argument but big fights need big energy, and they were both very tired. They lay at opposite sides of the burrow and went into a deep sleep for a very long time.

While they slept, the argument shriveled to a size small enough to resemble a joke. They woke up in a cheerful mood, laughing about two helpless helpers, and then they went out for a long wither to look for food.

Truth

orcupine was a carrier of desert secrets. He often waddled past the burrow and, if Snake and Lizard were at home, he would tell them the latest news. On this particular morning, Lizard saw him coming. 'Hi Porcupine! What's the latest?'

Porcupine sniffed the air. 'Snake not home yet?'

'She's seeing a client,' said Lizard, 'a duck who lost her nest in the big wind.'

'I know she went out,' Porcupine said. He came closer and cleared his throat. 'I saw her. But she wasn't with any duck. She was—how do I put it?—talking—to a snake.'

'No,' Lizard replied. 'She told me—it was a poor young duck that needed help.'

Porcupine had a shine in his eyes and a gossipy twitch at the corner of his mouth. 'You think I don't

know the difference between a snake and a duck?' he said.

This was one of those times when Lizard thought Porcupine an interfering old busybody. 'You'll have to excuse me,' he replied. 'I have clients this morning.'

Actually, his morning was quite empty. He went back into the burrow and filled in the waiting time imagining how the next conversation with Snake might begin.

I think Porcupine is getting soft in the head.

Do you know what that silly old Porcupine said?

How was that sad little duck? (Had that duck really lost her nest in the storm?)

Did the duck keep her appointment with you? (Was there a duck?)

What's all this about a snake? (Why did you lie to me?)

The suspicions became so real in Lizard's head, they were like memories, so when Snake slid into the burrow, he wasn't sure if he had anything left to say.

Snake spoke first, 'Hi Lizard! That's my first client of the day.'

Lizard said quietly, 'Did she pay you?'

Snake hesitated. 'No. Poor Duck. I told you—she lost everything.'

Lizard nodded. Snake was in such a good mood that he could not accuse her of lying. Not yet. He said, 'I've been wondering about something—'

'What?'

'Remember you told me how there was truth in a made-up story? What if a story doesn't have any truth in it?'

Snake wriggled. 'I don't know what you're talking about.'

Lizard went on, 'If a story has truth in it, it's a good story—right? If it doesn't have truth, it's a lie.'

Snake shook her head. 'This isn't the time for deep questions. Let's go and find some lunch.'

'A lie is a bad story,' Lizard insisted. 'Wouldn't you agree?'

'Oh, Lizard! Come on! We can talk about this later.'

Lizard refused to move. 'There should never be lies between friends,' he said.

Snake stopped. 'Oh, I get it! Porcupine!'

'So you were with a snake,' Lizard said. 'Who was he?'

'He's a she,' Snake replied. 'She's my distant cousin— distant as in living far away.'

Lizard gave Snake an accusing look. 'There was no poor little duck. You lied to me.'

Snake did a U-turn and slid back to Lizard. 'Remember your Sister Forty-Nine who heard that you and I were friends? How she came a long way to see us? Likewise my cousin.'

Lizard shook his head. 'Not like! Not wise! My Sister Forty-Nine came to our home and saw us both. You met your cousin out there in the desert on your own!'

'Lizard, she wanted to meet you! That's why she came, and that's why I arranged a meeting far away from here. I made up the story about the duck because I didn't want you to find out.'

'You were ashamed of me!'

'No, Buddy!' Snake put her nose against his. 'My cousin eats lizards.'

Lizard jumped back. 'She does?'

'Yes!' The word was almost a hiss. 'She loves

plump lizards as much as I love chicken eggs.'

Lizard gasped and was unable to speak.

'She's gone back home now, and you're quite safe. We can go out for lunch.'

As they withered side by side along the flat track by the burrow, Lizard said, 'Snake, I've been thinking about truth and story.'

'Not again!' said Snake.

'I just wanted to comment on the story about the duck.'

'There was no duck.'

'Yes, I know,' said Lizard. 'It had no truth in it, but all the same, it was a good story. Don't you think it was good?'

'I can't think when I'm hungry,' Snake replied.

Coyote

Snake once saw a horse crossing the desert with a human thing on its back. The horse's feet made a sound that Snake had never forgotten, and now the noise slipped into her dreams, ka-boom, ka-boom, ka-boom. In the dream, the horse's hooves were throwing sand into her face. She turned her head and woke up.

The burrow was lit by a shaft of gray morning

light, and small pebbles and dirt were falling from the roof.

'Lizard! Help!'

He was already awake, nose pointed up, and head twitching from side to side. 'It's directly above us!'

'A horse stamping on our burrow!' she gasped.

'No, not a horse. Listen!'

Ka-boom, ka-boom, a short silence and it started again. Ka-boom. Dirt fell on them like hard rain.

'I'm going out to look,' said Lizard.

'Do be careful!' Snake warned.

Boldly, bravely, Lizard scampered up the passageway to the entrance. He returned even faster, his eyes big with alarm. 'It's a coyote! She's sitting on top of us!'

'Coyote?' Snake was puzzled. 'Coyotes don't make that kind of noise.'

'She's scratching herself.'

'Scratching?'

'Do you have to question everything I say?' snapped Lizard. 'Yes, she's scratching. Because the earth is hollow, the sound is very loud and, I might say, very annoying.'

Snake wanted to ask another question but decided to rephrase it. 'I wonder why she's there.'

'I didn't stop to ask,' Lizard replied.

'Very wise,' said Snake, remembering that, recently, a hungry coyote had dug up a rabbit burrow.

'We can't go out until she leaves,' Lizard said.

Neither of them was happy to spend the morning crouched in a burrow guarded by a coyote who frequently sounded like a galloping horse. In a low voice, Lizard explained to Snake that creatures with fur got fleas that bit their skin. Scratching was their way of getting rid of fleas.

'It's not very successful,' said Snake, spitting out dirt that had fallen into her mouth.

Often, when Snake and Lizard were in the burrow and awake, they told each other stories, but today they were too tense, too afraid to raise their voices. Snake was not convinced that the coyote was scratching herself. She feared that the animal was digging her way into their burrow for a snack of Snake and Lizard.

'If that was her intention,' whispered Lizard, 'she would be digging at one of the entrances. She wouldn't try to come down through our ceiling.'

Snake was not certain, nor did she think Lizard was sure. She had learned that when her friend was afraid, he became grumpy. Like now.

The coyote stopped scratching. The dirt stopped falling. But she was still up there. They could hear her breathing, and every now and then she whined. What was she waiting for?

Snake could not bear the waiting. She turned to Lizard, 'Do you want to tell stories?'

'Not really,' he replied.

'It—it would help pass the time.'

'All right,' said Lizard. 'But cheerful stories. Stories that make us laugh. You start.'

Snake was quiet.

'I said, you start!'

'I can't think of any,' she whispered.

'Then I'll start. I'll make up a joke,' Lizard closed his eyes. 'What is the difference between a flea and a snake?'

'I beg your pardon?'

'You heard me—the difference between a flea and a snake!'

'That's what I thought you said. I don't know.'

Lizard smiled. 'A snake crawls on its own stomach.'

Snake was still for a moment. She said, 'That's not funny. It's not even cheerful.'

'You have no sense of humor, Snake,' said Lizard. He would have said more but the noise happened again, ka-boom, ka-boom, ka-boom. Lizard crouched as low as Snake on the floor of the burrow as dirt fell. The scratching stopped and the coyote barked. 'You guys! Helper and Helper! You awake down there?'

Snake and Lizard rushed to each other and lay side

by side, trembling. The coyote shifted slightly and growled.

After a long time, Snake whispered to Lizard, 'I know a joke.'

'What?' Lizard whispered back.

Snake put her mouth against Lizard's ear. 'Why is a coyote big and brown and furry?'

'I don't know,' he replied.

'Because if it was small and gray and smooth, it would be a lizard.'

Lizard moved away from her. 'You call that a joke?' he yelled. 'It's the stupidest thing I've ever heard!'

There was a stirring above their heads and the coyote barked again. 'Lizard! Is that you? I've been waiting for you guys to wake up!'

Helper and Helper

izard and Snake huddled in the burrow while the coyote barked, 'You're the Helpers—right? Well, get on out of there! I need some help!'

'It could be a trick,' whispered Snake.

Lizard agreed. 'Coyotes can be very economical with the truth,' he replied. 'But I have an idea.' He looked at the roof of the burrow and called, 'Coyote? Come around to our main entrance.'

The coyote gave a rumbling growl. 'Do I have to?'

'Yes, I'm afraid you do.'

'I've got a sore paw. Walking hurts.'

Snake leaned closer to Lizard. 'Sore paw! She can scratch, so why can't she walk?'

'Which paw?' Lizard yelled.

'Front.'

That satisfied Lizard. 'All right. Limp to the main entrance and we'll talk to you.'

There was another growl. 'Talking's no good. I want you to pull out the cactus thorn in my foot.'

Snake nudged Lizard. 'Tell her that we're the talking Helpers. Not the other kind.'

'We'll stay in the burrow,' whispered Lizard. 'If it is a trick, we'll be quite safe. She might have a thorn. We can possibly be useful.'

The coyote sat outside the doorway, blocking almost all the light. Her head was down on her paws and her pale yellow eyes watched as Lizard and Snake came toward her. Lizard stopped beyond reach, and Snake stopped behind Lizard.

Lizard said, 'Listen to me, Coyote. Push your paw

into the burrow. As far as it will go.'

The coyote understood. 'You think I'm going to bite you?'

Snake realized that Lizard was not taking any risks, and this made her bold. 'Do as Lizard says!' she ordered.

'How do I know YOU won't bite ME?' the coyote asked.

'Because we are Helpers,' Snake said coldly.

The coyote edged closer and pushed her leg, as far as the middle joint, into the hole. The burrow filled with coyote smell, a taste that warned Snake's tongue of danger, but even with her dim sight she could see that the paw pad was swollen.

Lizard sniffed at the coyote's foot. 'You've got a cactus spine stuck between your toes.'

'I know that!' barked Coyote.

'I can try to pull it out,' Lizard said.

Because the rest of Coyote was blocking the entrance, Lizard had to work by touch rather than sight. Each time his claws slid over the end of the thorn, Coyote yelped and flinched with pain. Lizard grunted with effort but the cactus thorn stayed stuck firmly in the foot.

'Let me try,' murmured Snake.

'How?' Lizard wanted to know.

Snake slid forward until her nose was against the poor sore paw. She felt the swelling and heat of it, and tasted the hurt.

Then she came to the hard thorn that stuck out like an extra claw. She opened her mouth and wedged the end of the thorn between her fangs.

'Ow, ow, ow!' howled Coyote.

Snake slid backward and the thorn came out.

Coyote pulled her leg out of the hole and licked her paw. 'It's gone! You did it! You guys are great! Look!' She stood up, paw on the ground. 'I can walk! I can run! Oh, whoopee-do! I'll be right back with your payment. What is it? Still quails' eggs and beetles?' She wagged her tail and loped off.

'Well done, Snake,' Lizard said admiringly. 'You have just proved that Lizard and Snake, Helper and Helper, can do more than give advice. 'Quails' eggs and beetles, eh? I wonder how many.'

Snake sighed. 'Lithard?'

'What?'

'I need thum help.'

Lizard looked at her. 'Is something wrong?'

'Yeth,' said Snake. 'There'th a cactuth thorn thtuck in my fangth.'

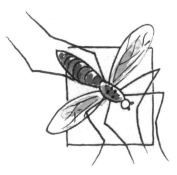

Frog

Lizard sometimes had bad dreams that made him twitch and squeak in his sleep. This seemed odd to Snake, for in waking times, Lizard was the braver and bolder of the two. After one such twitchy night, Lizard went into a deep sleep at dawn and didn't wake in time for the morning food hunt in the desert.

Snake decided that the wither would have to be

a slither, and quietly, so as not to disturb him, she left the burrow.

To her astonishment, there, by the door, sat a fat green frog.

Snake had pleasant memories of frogs. Unfortunately, those experiences had been few, for the simple reason that frogs lived in water. Snake knew there were snakes who were at home in water, but she was not one of them. She disliked water. To tell the truth, she had been terrified of it ever since she and Lizard had fallen in the river and been swept away. She stared at the frog, her tongue flickering, her mouth filling with juice.

The frog stared back with bulging eyes as yellow as the sun. It made no attempt to hop away. Why was the creature so far from its watery home?

Snake's jaw unhinged by itself and before she could answer her own question, the frog was sliding head first into her stomach. It barely struggled. Snake sighed, unable to believe her luck. Breakfast had been served outside her own front door.

As was usual after a large meal, she felt sleepy. Instead of the morning slither, she went back into the burrow, coiled up near Lizard and was soon asleep.

She woke much later with Lizard shouting in her ear. 'Get up, Snake. Please, get up. We're very late!'

'I've already been up,' she protested. 'You were asleep so I went back to bed.'

'Did you see him?' Lizard asked.

'Who?'

'My client. He was supposed to come this morning.'

Snake stifled a small burp and said again, 'Who?' although she had already guessed.

'Frog,' said Lizard. 'He had a problem and I said we'd talk about it. I don't suppose you caught sight—'

'He's gone,' said Snake, trying to be truthful.

'I told him to wait,' Lizard complained.

'You were asleep for a very long time.'

'I know, I know. I suppose I'd better find him and make another appointment.'

Snake slowly stretched. 'I wouldn't do that, if I were you. I got the impression he wasn't coming back.'

'Why? What did he say?'

'He didn't say anything. It was more a feeling I had.'

Lizard stopped fidgeting. 'Oh Snake, did you scare him away?'

'Of course not.' Snake searched for truth. 'He was a friendly frog. I felt very close to him. Tell me, what was his problem?'

'His voice,' Lizard replied. 'It's mating season and he's supposed to sing to the female frogs. Trouble is, he hasn't learned to croak.'

Snake curled her tail over the bulge in her stomach. He's croaked now, she thought, and she closed her eyes to avoid further conversation.

Flies

As the days grew longer, the river became narrower, shrinking in the heat to a brown trickle, leaving pools of wet mud between the stones. Small flies gathered above these stones, a mass of insects so thick that it became a buzzing black cloud.

Lizard looked forward to the fly season. When it came, the morning wither went by the river where

Snake watched while Lizard leaped about on his hind legs, snapping at the insects above his head.

Snake couldn't see the point of so much effort for so little reward. 'They're like specks of dust,' she said.

'But they are delicious, Snake,' said Lizard, 'rare little morsels that come only once a year.'

Snake sniffed. 'I'm surprised you get enough to taste.'

'I would catch more if you weren't so impatient,' Lizard said. 'No sooner do I start eating than you want to go.'

Snake replied, 'That's because I'm afraid you'll fall and hurt yourself—all that leaping about like a flea on a hot stone.'

'The stone is quite cool,' Lizard replied. 'I'll have you know it is not flea behavior. Catching river flies is what lizards have been doing since the beginning of time. If you don't want to watch, you can always go for a slither on your own.'

Snake saw no point in arguing since Lizard always had to have the last word, but the next morning, while Lizard was jumping up and down with an open

mouth, Snake quietly slithered away to another part of
the river where a pair of ducks had a late batch of eggs
among some reeds.

Much later, Lizard met Snake at the burrow. He
was jittery with anger. 'I looked for you! I hunted
all over!'

'You told me to go off on my own,' Snake said.

'I gave you an option,' Lizard cried. 'It was up to you to tell me you were going to take it. You're supposed to be my friend.'

Snake said calmly, 'Lizard, it's because I'm your friend that I can't bear to watch that stupid fly dance. It's very dangerous. You could fall. Why do it? There are bigger and better bugs to be had under the mesquite bushes.'

Lizard glared. 'I thought we had agreed not to talk about each other's eating habits.'

Snake corrected him. 'You agreed not to mention the way I eat eggs.'

'Egg eating, fly catching, what's the difference?'

Snake thought for a moment and had to agree that Lizard was right. She said, 'You know what bothers me? It's that we can't talk about these things. You're my best friend. I'm your best friend. We should be able to talk about anything, anything at all, because that's the way it is with friends.'

Lizard lost his anger. He put his head near Snake's. 'Yes, Snake. Oh yes, indeed! Sometimes we forget that. We are the greatest of friends and nothing should be hidden between us. Do tell me! I don't mind! Why did you slither off on your own this morning?'

'I've already told you, Lizard. It's because I can't bear to see you doing something so dangerous.'

Lizard shook his head. 'If you really thought it was dangerous, you would stay in case I needed help. Isn't that true?'

Snake closed her mouth. 'All right,' she said at last. 'I'll tell you. I can't bear to watch you because you look ridiculous.'

Lizard sat up tall. 'Ridiculous?'

'Yes.'

With a great swish of his tail, Lizard turned and stomped out of the burrow. Snake followed him, calling, 'Where are you going?'

He yelled at her, 'Down to the river to catch more flies!'

'All right,' she yelled back. 'But if you fall and break your legs, don't come running to me for help.'

Balloon

The afternoon breeze sometimes brought strange things from other places, plastic bags that hung in the bushes like discarded snakeskins, and newspapers that tore themselves to bits on cactus thorns.

One day, a blue balloon was tugged across the sky. At sunset, as the wind dropped, the balloon drifted down, down, toward Snake and Lizard.

The friends had been withering along, lost in a marvelous conversation about ancestors, when Lizard looked up and gave a great gasp. 'Oh Snake! A sky egg!'

Snake, unable to see well, didn't know what he was talking about.

'It's beautiful!' Lizard cried. 'Round and shining blue! It's coming this way!' He jumped up, squeaking with excitement. 'Yes, yes! Can you see it now?'

Snake was aware of something moving above her and her tongue flickered nervously, but there was no taste of danger in the air. Without a sound, a round blue thing bounced on the ground and lay in front of her, trembling slightly. Snake's caution was replaced with awe. Lizard was right. It was an egg from the sky. She touched it with her nose and it wobbled. 'It's very light,' she said.

'Of course it is! Sky eggs are as light as air. They are full of spirit.' Lizard walked slowly around the balloon. 'Snake, oh Snake, why did it come to us?'

Snake didn't know. Her head filled with stories of the great Sky Serpent who laid the sun egg each

morning. 'I think,' she said, 'it's a Sky Serpent egg.'

'No, no,' Lizard was definite. 'You said yourself that the Sky Serpent egg is hot and yellow. My ancestor the Sky Dragon eats the sun egg every night and every morning the Sky Serpent lays another.'

Snake had an idea. 'Sky Serpent and Sky Dragon work together to make days and nights, so maybe they made this egg together.'

Lizard's eyes shone. 'Snake, you are a genius! This is a Sky Dragent egg!'

'Sky Serpon, Buddy,' Snake said.

'It has chosen us from all the creatures in the desert!' he exclaimed. 'What an honor! What a privilege!'

'I wonder why?' Snake touched the blue ball again. Its skin was soft and quite warm.

'Maybe Sky Dragon and Sky Serpent want us to look after it until it hatches,' Lizard said. 'Maybe they had heard that we are Helpers.'

This was story, they both knew it, and yet the story contained so much truth, they were overcome with feelings of pride and responsibility.

'It's too big to take home,' Snake said.

'We'll roll it close to our burrow, then we'll take turns to sit outside and guard it. Come on, Snake. It'll be dark soon.'

Gently nudging the blue ball with their noses, they guided it back toward the burrow. At the bottom of the slope that led to their front door, they lost control and the Sky Egg slipped sideways. Lizard stood on his hind legs and gripped it firmly between his claws.

BANG!

The noise was so loud they thought the world had come to an end. Blind with fear, they rushed to their burrow and, side by side, squeezed through the entrance. They fled down the tunnel and lay panting in a warm hollow of safety.

'What happened?' Snake whispered.

'I don't know. Listen!'

They held their breath to hear better, but there was no further sound outside.

'We can't stay here,' Lizard reminded Snake. 'We've been chosen to guard the egg.'

'You go first,' Snake whispered.

Slowly, they moved up the tunnel and Lizard

poked his head out the entrance. 'It's gone.'

'Gone? Where?'

'Maybe it went back to the sky because we abandoned it.' Lizard's voice was sad.

'Or maybe a coyote got it,' said Snake.

They came out of the burrow and looked around. The earth was moving into darkness and the orange sunset had paled to yellow. There was no sign of the Sky Egg.

Lizard was now very upset. He walked back and forth, swishing his tail in the dust. 'It came to us! It needed help and—and we left it.'

Snake tried to comfort him. 'There was a loud noise.'

'Maybe a rock falling somewhere. Did we stay by the Sky Egg? Did we protect it? No, Snake, we did not. First hint of danger, we ran away.'

Snake slithered down the slope, tongue flickering, trying to pick up the taste of a predator that might have taken the Sky Egg. She slid over something soft and drew back. 'Lizard?'

'Yes?'

'What's this? It tastes like the Sky Egg.'

Lizard bounded down the slope and his sobbing was suddenly replaced by a shriek of excitement. 'It has hatched! Snake, this is the egg skin! Our Sky Egg has hatched!'

Snake peered into the darkness, fearing strange sky creatures in every shadow. 'Where is it?'

'Gone back to the sky where it belongs. Oh yes! I understand it now, Snake. It only came down to us because it needed help to break out of its egg.'

Snake thought for a moment. 'That noise. Was that the hatching?'

'Of course!' said Lizard. 'The egg couldn't hatch without us!'

Snake thought for another moment. 'Is this story? Or is it true?'

'It is both, one hundred percent,' said Lizard.

At that moment, a coyote howled nearby, warning them of the dangers of the night. Lizard picked up the piece of soft blue rubber, went back to the burrow and laid it gently in the corner.

The friends talked long into the night. 'I'm wondering,' said Snake, 'just how we helped the Sky Egg to hatch.'

'It's a mystery,' said Lizard. 'The laws of Sky are different from the laws of Earth. What we do know is that it chose us. Us, dear Snake! The egg of the

Sky Dragent crossed the boundary between Sky and Earth to ask Lizard and Snake, Helper and Helper, for assistance.'

· 'Serpon,' said Snake. 'Sky Serpon.'

Lizard was in a generous mood. 'It doesn't matter,' he said. 'It's story.'

'But true,' said Snake.

'Absolutely true!'

Snake said slowly, 'Does this mean that every time someone tells a story about the Sky Serpent and the Sky Dragon, we'll be in it?'

Lizard laughed with pure pleasure. 'Of course! Dear Snake, this is a great event and we should celebrate. Let's have an extra big supper!'

Snake moved toward the back of the burrow where she had a small heap of fresh quails' eggs given to her by a grateful armadillo. That, however, had been this morning. Much had happened since then. A slow feeling of sorrow came over her. 'I can't,' she said.

'Can't what?' Lizard wanted to know.

'Eat eggs,' she explained. 'They are sacred. They hold life. Lizard, we were chosen to be egg protectors.

That means—' She struggled to say it. 'I can never eat eggs again.'

'What a lot of nonsense!' said Lizard.

'It isn't nonsense. It's story and it's true.' Snake mournfully flicked her tongue over the smell of fresh egg. 'These are the quail of the future. They have been laid to grow into my friends, not my food—' The last word was lost in a puddle of saliva.

Lizard lost patience with her. As he crunched a beetle, he said, 'That's quite enough, Snake! Shut your mouth and eat your supper.'

DATE DUE

AP 1 4 '12		
JE 1 5 '17		
JE 1 4 '12		
JE 2 8 '12		
AG 0 6 '12		
OC 0 2 '12		
FE 0 3 '13		
GAYLORD		PRINTED IN U.S.A.